Visit us on the Web! www.randomhouse.com/kids
Educators and librarians, for a variety of teaching tools, visit us at www.randomhouse.com/teachers

Library of Congress Cataloging-in-Publication Data
Huget, Jennifer LaRue.
The best birthday party ever / Jennifer LaRue Huget; illustrated by LeUyen Pham.—1st ed.
p. cm.
Summary: A child plans an elaborate birthday party and eagerly counts the months,
days, hours, and minutes before the celebration.
ISBN 978-0-375-84763-9 (trade) — ISBN 978-0-375-95763-5 (lib. bdg.)
[1. Birthdays—Fiction. 2. Parties—Fiction.] I. Pham, LeUyen, ill. II. Title.
PZ7.H872958Bs 2010
[E]—dc22
2009028010

The text of this book is set in Granjon.
The illustrations were rendered in watercolor.
Book design by Rachael Cole

MANUFACTURED IN CHINA
10 9 8 7 6 5 4 3 2 1
First Edition

For Sophie Jane
Huget, who has
always loved a
birthday party,
no matter whose
it is. —J.L.H.

To Miele, the
ultimate party
dinosaur. —L.P.

The Best Birthday Party Ever

by Jennifer LaRue Huget

illustrated by LeUyen Pham

COME TO CIRCUS

PARTY STARTS HERE

My birthday is **5** months, **3** weeks, **2** days, and **8** hours away.

Today I started to plan my party.

It is going to be the best birthday party ever.

I will make the invitations myself.
They will have a picture of me
dressed like a princess on the front.

My mother will help me color them
in. We will put gold glitter in the
envelopes so when people open them
they'll get showered with fairy dust.

you're
Invited!

I am inviting all my friends—57 of them, counting some kids I just met at the grocery store.

Plus my grandmas.

And the mailman.

And the lady at the bank who gives me lollipops.

My birthday
will be here in

4 MONTHS

2 WEEKS

5 DAYS

and 7 HOURS

We will have 9 thousand balloons at my party. All pink. And pink streamers. And pink napkins. And pink ice cream. Or maybe they'll be chartreuse.

Everybody will get to eat 7 scoops of ice cream. And there will be hot fudge sauce and strawberry syrup and whipped cream and rainbow sprinkles and cherries for the top.

Before we cut the cake, everybody will sing "Happy Birthday" to me.

It will be so loud my grandmas will have to cover their ears.

My birthday is

3 months,

1 week,

3 days, and

7 hours from now.

I will have the tallest
cake in the world—
17 layers. Every layer
will be a different flavor.
The cake will be so tall
that I will have to stand
on a ladder to cut it.

There will also be 17 colors of frosting. Plus extra you can eat right out of the bowl.

There will be 6 zillion candles on top. We will have to warn the fire department before we light them.

When I blow out the candles, I will get to make 6 zillion wishes. One for every candle.

There will also be
a magician named Merlin.

And another magician, too, just in case the first one cuts himself in half or makes himself disappear or something. And when they do that trick where they take a bunny out of a hat, I get to keep the bunny.

Speaking of hats, every girl will get to wear a real tiara instead of a paper party hat. And the boys will get clown hats with bells on them. My mother will make them.

For party favors we will give every guest a hamster.

Only

2 Months
1 week
6 Days
& 4 Hours

left until my birthday.

After cake and ice cream we will all jump around in a giant moon bounce shaped like a castle. And nobody will get sick.

Or maybe we can have a real castle with towers and a drawbridge. My dad knows how to build things like that.

There could also be a moat. With goldfish. And a serpent.

Of course we will have pony rides.

No, wait—camels.

Or elephants.

And maybe
a Ferris wheel.

1 month 2 weeks 4 days 9 HOURS

until the best birthday party ever!

I believe the President of the United States will send me a birthday card that we can read out loud at my party. And so will the Queen of England. After my party I will frame those cards and hang them on my wall. I will make a collage with all the other birthday cards I get. It will be so big I will probably have to tape it to my ceiling because it won't fit anywhere else.

You know how sometimes at a parade they have fighter jets fly over, and it looks like they're so close together their wings are touching? We're having that at my party. The planes will be so loud my grandmas will have to cover their ears again.

I hope the hamsters don't get scared.

Now that I think about it, a parade sounds like fun.

We can put all my presents on a float so everyone can get a good look at them. And I can sit on top of the pile and wave at everyone. Like a princess. And maybe I could throw sparkly necklaces and candy into the crowd.

And if we're having a
parade, maybe we should
have fireworks, too.

Mom says this birthday
party of mine is getting a
little bit out of hand.
Okay, maybe we can skip
the sparkly necklaces.

Tomorrow is my birthday.

All this planning has tired me out.

Mom kissed me and told me to get a good
night's sleep, because tomorrow's my Big Day.

Today is my birthday!

Of course, not everyone could come to my party.

There are no hamsters for favors.

There is also no Ferris wheel. Or moon bounce.

There don't seem to be any elephants, either.

The President's card didn't arrive yet. Neither did the Queen's.

And I guess the magicians couldn't make it after all.

The balloons are all pink, and so are the napkins and the streamers.

My cake has two layers, both the same flavor.

But they're chocolate, with strawberry frosting!
My very favorite!

And Mom made extra frosting so I could eat
some right out of the bowl.

Everybody sang "Happy Birthday" so loud,
we *all* had to cover our ears!

I made 7 wishes. One for each candle,
plus one for good luck.

And guess what I got for a present?

A bunny!

I'm having the best birthday party ever.

Just like I planned.